Midnight Magic

Amy Gordon

illustrated by Judy Clifford

little rainbow®

Troll

Published by Little Rainbow,
an imprint and trademark of Troll Communications L.L.C.

First published in hardcover by BridgeWater Books.

Printed in the United States of America.

10   9   8   7   6   5   4   3   2   1

Library of Congress Cataloging-in-Publication Data

Lawson, Amy.
Midnight Magic / by Amy Gordon; illustrated by Judy Clifford.
p.   cm.
Summary: While Uncle Harry is babysitting his nephews for the
weekend, the Tooth Fairy leaves a gold key meant for the Ogre in
Puss in Boots.
ISBN 0-8167-3660-X (lib.)   ISBN 0-8167-3661-8 (pbk.)
[1. Brothers—Fiction.   2. Uncles—Fiction.   3. Tooth Fairy—
Fiction.]   I. Clifford, Judy, ill.   II. Title.
PZ7.L438228Un   1995   [Fic]   94-34967

To Nick, Nate, Jules, and Hugh.
A.G.

For my son, Nicky, whose image
graces these pages and whose
spirit inspires me.
J.C.

CHAPTER
ONE

It was the day their mother and father were leaving for the weekend. Uncle Harry was going to come stay with them. Jake and Sam fought all morning long.

Jake wanted to go by himself out to the workshop to get clean wood shavings for his hamsters. "Why can't I go with you?" Sam, Jake's younger brother, pleaded.

"Because you're not big enough," Jake replied.

"I *am* big," said Sam.

"You aren't big. You haven't even lost any teeth yet."

"I almost have," said Sam, wiggling one of his front teeth. "It's loose."

Jake stomped off, past the pile of suitcases waiting by the kitchen door. Sam began to howl. "Why can't I go with him? He never lets me go with him."

His mother put down the pile of clean clothes she was trying to fold before leaving and wrapped her arms around him. "Sam, please try to get along with Jake while we're away," she said.

Jake returned with a bulging paper bag and tromped back past the suitcases, leaving a trail of sawdust behind him.

"Jake," said his father, who was looking at a map spread out on the kitchen table, "why do you have to do this *now?*"

"I *have* to," Jake said. "The hamsters will die if I don't clean out their cage right now."

He lifted off the lid of the cage and put the two fat, orangey-brown hamsters in the sink.

"Watch them," Jake ordered Sam. "Don't let them get away."

Sam scraped a chair across the kitchen floor and pushed it against the counter so he could stand watch over the hamsters.

Then Jake picked up the hamster cage, which was full of old shavings, and turned it upside down over the mouth of another paper bag. About half the shavings landed in the bag. The other half landed on the floor.

"Jake," said his father again. "Do you really have to do this now?"

"Do you think the Ogre could turn into a hamster?" asked Sam. "If he could turn into a mouse, he could turn into a hamster, couldn't he?"

"You and your Ogre," said Jake, dumping new shavings into the cage. "Mom, is Uncle Harry going to have to read *Puss in Boots* every night while you're away? Can't Sam listen to something else for a change?"

"Speaking of Uncle Harry . . ." his mother began.

"Here I am! Hello, everyone!" Uncle Harry strode into the kitchen.

Uncle Harry was Jake and Sam's mother's younger brother. He was an actor, a very good one. He had a rich, deep voice that filled all the corners of the room.

"Well, I guess it's time for us to go, boys," their mother said. "We know you'll have a wonderful time with Uncle Harry."

She put on her coat. Their father folded up the map and carried the suitcases out to the car.

And just as Sam's mother was kissing him good-bye, Sam's first tooth fell out.

And just as their mother and father's car drove out of the driveway, Jake discovered that his hamsters were no longer in the sink.

CHAPTER
TWO

Sam walked around the kitchen, poking at the bloody hole in his mouth. "The Tooth Fairy won't come!" he moaned. "She won't come if Mommy and Daddy aren't here!"

Jake roamed the kitchen. "I'll never find them!" he cried. "Frisky and Lazy are gone forever." Jake had named his hamsters Frisky and Lazy because, although they looked exactly alike, their personalities couldn't have been more different.

"Well," Uncle Harry finally said. "There are two things that always cheer *me* up."

Sam stopped moaning. Jake circled Uncle Harry like a shark.

"One of them is food," Uncle Harry said.

"Tonight, we will have Slumgoni. Or would you prefer Tuna Wiggle?"

Sam brought the finger out of his mouth. Jake moved in closer.

"Tuna Wiggle?" Jake asked.

"Tuna Wiggle," Uncle Harry said, wiggling.

"Tuna Wiggle," said Sam with a giggle.

"Tuna Wiggle, Tuna Wiggle, Tuna Wiggle!" All three began to chant, marching in a circle, wiggling as they went.

"Tuna Wiggle," Uncle Harry sang, opening a can of tuna fish. "Macaroni," he continued, opening the pantry door and poking about the shelves. "You can't have Tuna Wiggle without macaroni. Boys, where's the macaroni?"

"Macaroni, macaroni," the boys shouted with glee.

"Ah, macaroni," said Uncle Harry, pulling the box from the shelf. "Tuna Wiggle went to town, riding on a pony, put a jiggle in his cap, and called it Macaroni!"

Jake and Sam fell to the floor, laughing. Jake began to tickle Sam. Uncle Harry stirred macaroni and cheese and tuna fish all together in a pot on the stove.

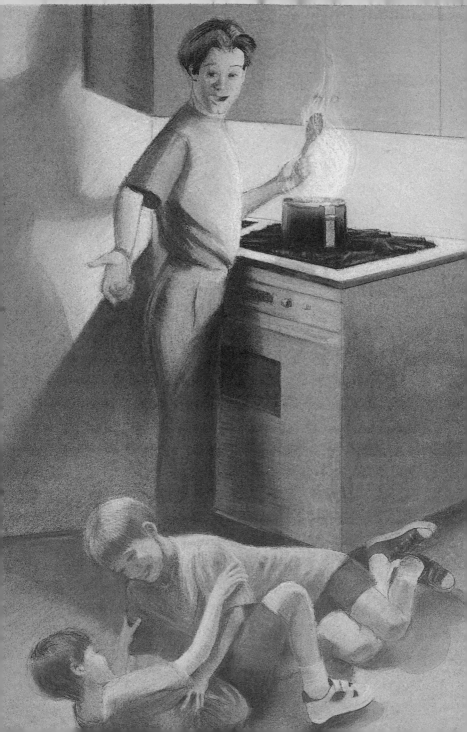

"Stop!" screamed Sam. "Stop tickling me!"

"Ready to eat!" Uncle Harry sang out.

He scooped up three servings of Tuna Wiggle and set them on the table.

"This is really delicious," Uncle Harry pronounced after the first mouthful.

But Sam suddenly dropped his fork and began to howl.

"You don't like Tuna Wiggle, Sam?" Uncle Harry asked with concern.

"My tooth!" said Sam. "I lost my tooth!" He flung himself off the chair and onto the floor.

"My hamsters!" cried Jake, flinging himself off *his* chair.

"O Tuna Wiggle, I shall not forget thee, though I leave thee at this lonely hour," said Uncle Harry. He joined the boys in their scramble across the floor.

"Frisky! Lazy!" Jake called.

Uncle Harry searched with his nose to the floor. "The tooth, as I remember it, is barely visible to the human eye."

"I found it!" Sam screamed suddenly. He held out the tiniest speck of Something.

"It might be his tooth. Or it might be a piece

of dried-up macaroni," Uncle Harry said quietly to himself.

"My tooth, my tooth," Sam said lovingly. He handed it to Uncle Harry. "You hold it so I don't lose it."

"I can't find them," Jake wailed. "Frisky and Lazy probably got outside. They'll be eaten, or they'll starve to death, and I'll never see them again!"

"Hamsters have a way of turning up. You just wait and see," said Uncle Harry. "Now come on, everyone. I can hear the Tuna Wiggle calling us. 'Come back to me, boys, come back to me.'"

At the mention of Tuna Wiggle, Jake and Sam returned to the table.

CHAPTER
THREE

"What's the second thing that cheers you up, Uncle Harry?" asked Jake after the Tuna Wiggle feast.

"The second thing that cheers me up is reading aloud."

"*Puss in Boots*," yelled Sam.

"No!" Jake groaned. "We have to listen to that story every single night!"

"Ah, but you have never *seen* it," said Uncle Harry, leaping to his feet. "I will now perform *Puss in Boots* for you! But pajamas on first, please."

"It's not my bedtime," Jake protested.

"If you're going to be an audience, you have to wear audience clothes. This evening, those clothes happen to be pajamas," said Uncle Harry.

"But . . ."

"You'll be turned away at the door," said Uncle Harry. "Curtain goes up in three minutes."

In four and a half minutes, Jake was in his blue pajamas and Sam was in his red ones. They sat on the bottom bunk bed with Uncle Harry between them.

"Once upon a time," Uncle Harry began in his deep voice.

And then he sprang to his feet and became the clever cat who strode about in high boots, managing to make a very fine life for his master, the miller's youngest son.

"Oh, goody!" Sam squealed when they got to the part where Puss walked up to the Ogre's castle door.

"Knock, knock, knock," said Uncle Harry, knocking on an imaginary door.

Then he whipped around, as though he were standing behind the door, and became the Ogre. "Yes?" he thundered in a deep voice. "Who goes there?"

"It is I, Puss," he answered in a smooth, velvety voice.

The Ogre let Puss into his castle. Puss said, "Is it true that you can turn into anything you want?"

"Of course," the Ogre said.

Sam's eyes—and Jake's, too—shone with delight as Uncle Harry turned into an elephant and then into a lion.

"And now he's going to turn into a mouse!" Sam shouted.

Uncle Harry *did* turn into a mouse. He crouched on the floor and his nose twitched and his whole body trembled as though he were about to be eaten by a cat.

"How does he do that?" asked Jake.

Before anyone could answer, Uncle Harry jumped up and became Puss again. With a graceful flick of his paw, he scooped up the mouse and ate it in one gulp.

"Very tasty," said Uncle Harry the cat, daintily cleaning his whiskers. "Almost as good as Tuna Wiggle."

Sam giggled, but Jake was quiet. "I kind of feel sorry for the Ogre," he said suddenly.

Uncle Harry and Sam stared at Jake.

"The Ogre hadn't done anything to hurt Puss

in Boots. So I don't see why he had to be eaten," Jake said.

"He had to be eaten because he was mean," said Sam with a yawn. He picked up his blanket and felt for the new hole where his tooth used to be. "All ogres are mean."

"But maybe he was mean for a reason," Jake argued. "Maybe he was in a bad mood because his boots were too tight and they hurt."

"You're silly," said Sam.

CHAPTER
FOUR

"What about my tooth?" Sam asked as Uncle Harry tucked him into bed. "Do you think the Tooth Fairy will come?"

"No," said Jake. "She won't come, because Mom and Dad aren't here."

"Why, Jake, I'm surprised at you," Uncle Harry said. "Don't you know that the Tooth Fairy does not need moms and dads? She comes and goes as she pleases."

He swooped down on Jake and tossed him up to the top bunk. "All the Tooth Fairy needs is the night, and for boys to be quiet—very, very quiet. So put your tooth under your pillow, Sam, and we'll turn out the light."

Uncle Harry turned out the light.

"Leave the door open and the hall light on," said Sam.

"It's not my bedtime," said Jake, sitting up on his bed.

"Then I'll sing until it is," said Uncle Harry. "O Tuna Wiggle, Macaroni, thank you for this day. O Tooth and Hamsters, we had lost you, but you are here to stay."

"Not the hamsters," said Jake.

"Not the hamsters," Uncle Harry agreed. "But I can't help thinking . . ."

"Go on with the song," said Sam.

"O Ogre, we are sorry to have eaten you all up. But maybe tomorrow we'll have something different for our sup. And sooooo, good night, good night."

"Good night, Uncle Harry," Sam called.

"I'm still not sleepy," said Jake. "It's my turn for a story, and not a baby one, either."

Uncle Harry thought for a moment. Then he hauled himself up to the top bunk and lay down next to Jake. His feet stuck out under the railing.

"You're squishing me," Jake complained.

"You're squishing *me*," said Uncle Harry. "Move over."

"Tell me a story about when you and Mom were kids," said Jake.

"Once, when your mom and I were kids," Uncle Harry began, "we had a white rat. His name was Rasputin. One day he escaped from his cage, and we couldn't find him anywhere."

"What happened?" asked Jake, lifting himself up on one elbow.

"Well, your mother had this idea. She thought if we drew a picture of Rasputin and stared and stared at it, Rasputin would sense us thinking about him. Then he would come back to us."

"Did that happen?" asked Jake.

"Yes."

Jake put his head down and yawned. "Maybe that's what I'll do."

Uncle Harry swung his long legs off the bunk bed. They almost touched the floor.

"Quiet, now. Sam is asleep, and the hour of the Tooth Fairy is upon us."

Jake yawned again. "Good night, Uncle Harry."

"Good night, Jake."

Jake pulled the covers up and thought very hard about his hamsters. His eyes closed.

And then Jake dreamed. He dreamed he saw a tall figure wearing a floppy hat and a robe standing near the bed. The figure bent over his brother.

Jake sat up and rubbed his eyes. He hung his head over the edge of the bed and looked at Sam. Sam was snoring. There was no one in a floppy hat and robe standing over him. It really had been a dream.

CHAPTER
FIVE

Jake opened his eyes. It was morning. Sam was squealing with excitement.

"Jake! Jake! She came! She really came!" Sam sped up the ladder of the bunk bed and scrambled over Jake's feet.

"Watch what you're doing!" Jake cried. "Ouch! Get off me!"

"The Tooth Fairy came! Look what she brought me!" Sam yelled. He opened his fingers.

In the palm of Sam's hand was a key. It was a small, old-fashioned key that might have belonged to a treasure chest.

"It's real gold," said Sam.

"Let me see it," said Jake. He grabbed at the key.

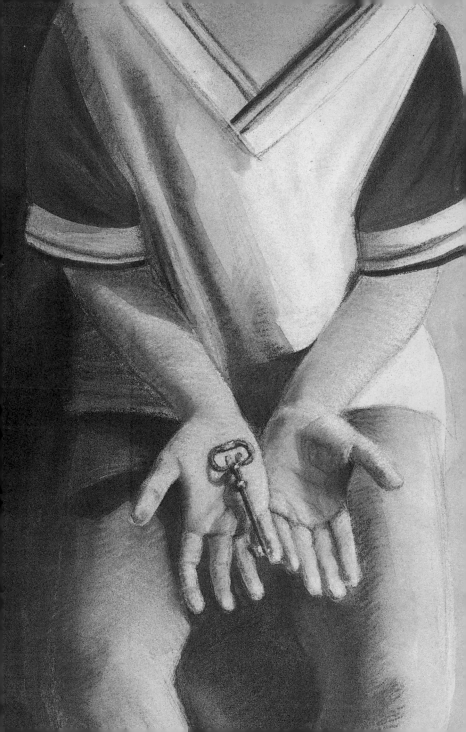

"It's mine," said Sam, quickly closing his fingers.

"I know it's yours. Just let me see it." Jake tried to pry Sam's fingers open.

"It's mine!" Sam howled as the key sailed through the air and fell to the ground.

Jake was off the bunk in a flash. He landed on top of the key.

"It *is* gold," Jake said, almost whispering. "You're so lucky. The Tooth Fairy never gave me anything like this."

Sam stopped crying. "I *am* lucky," he said cheerfully. He jumped off the bed. "I got a real gold key from the Tooth Fairy."

"I wonder why," said Jake. "Uncle Harry must know why. Let's go show it to him."

Sam grabbed the key. "I'll race you," he shouted.

Jake and Sam slid down the banister. Jake reached Uncle Harry's room first. "Uncle Harry!" he yelled.

Sam was close behind. "Uncle Harry!" He jumped on Uncle Harry's bed.

Uncle Harry sat up and shook his head. "Who is calling me in the middle of the night?"

"It's not the middle of the night," said Sam. He held the key in Uncle Harry's face. "Look at what the Tooth Fairy brought me."

"Zounds!" exclaimed Uncle Harry. "A key!"

"Don't act so surprised," said Jake.

"A gold key," said Sam.

"A gold key," Uncle Harry repeated.

"You're a good actor, Uncle Harry," said Jake.

"Please, Sam, may I hold it for a moment?" Uncle Harry asked.

Sam handed it over. "Be careful," he said.

"Of course," said Uncle Harry. "A gold key. On the morning after Tuna Wiggle, we have a gold key. But what did she say?"

"Who?" asked Sam.

"The Tooth Fairy. She must have left a note. You don't just leave a gold key under someone's pillow without leaving a note."

Jake and Sam flew off the bed. They were up the stairs in a flash. They found the Tooth Fairy's note at the same moment. Jake pulled one way. Sam pulled the other way. The note ripped in half.

Uncle Harry climbed the stairs when he

heard Sam screaming. He picked up the two halves of the note and held them together.

"'Dear Sam,'" he read. "'Please find the Ogre and return this key to him. He needs it very badly. Thank you very much. Your friend, the Tooth Fairy.'"

Jake and Sam and Uncle Harry looked at one another.

"Well," said Uncle Harry. "I guess we know what we're going to do today."

"What?" asked the boys.

"On the morning after Tuna Wiggle," Uncle Harry said in his deepest voice, "we are going to find the Ogre."

CHAPTER
SIX

"There's no such thing as an ogre," said Jake.

"Bagels over easy, piglets in a poke," sang Uncle Harry, standing over the stove in his pajamas. He was stirring bagels, sausages, and eggs in a pan.

"Bagels over easy," Sam repeated.

"They're really good for breakfast, and that's no joke," sang Uncle Harry.

"I'm going to draw a picture of Frisky and Lazy," said Jake. He found a piece of paper and a pencil and sat down at the table. "They look alike, but they act differently. I'll draw Frisky with his eyes open and Lazy all curled up in a ball."

"I hope we can find the Ogre," said Sam. "Maybe we should draw a picture of him, too."

Jake shaded in Frisky's stripes. "There's no such thing as an ogre," he said again. "And I know who wrote the note."

"Bagels over easy, piglets in a poke," Uncle Harry sang loudly. "This is very yummy, and that's no joke! And kids who don't believe in things are poor old folks! Sam, get me the salt, would you, my friend?"

Sam went to the counter to get the salt. In a moment, he was shouting. "Uncle Harry! I found some kind of map!"

Uncle Harry's jaw dropped open in astonishment. "Zounds!" he cried. "Can it be?"

Jake jumped up from the table. "Let me see!" he cried, grabbing for it.

"I found it!" yelled Sam, yanking it back.

"We're going to rip it," said Jake suddenly.

"Ah, good lad," said Uncle Harry. "Some people *can* learn a thing or two, I'm glad to see. Now what have we here?"

Jake and Sam and Uncle Harry spread the map out on the kitchen table next to Jake's drawing of the hamsters.

"What does it say? What does it say?" Sam asked, leaning over it.

"Move out of the way, and maybe I could tell you," said Jake. "It says 'Map for Finding Ogres.' It's a map of our yard. There's our house, and there's all the woods behind it."

"And there's our tree house," said Sam, pointing. "See, there's the big tree at the top of the hill, and there's a little tree house in it."

"The tree house has an X on it," said Jake.

"Do you think the Ogre is in there?" asked Sam, his eyes big.

"No."

"You mean, 'Oh, no!'" said Uncle Harry, leaping toward the stove. "The bagels are burning. Help, boys! The pigs are on fire!" He whisked the frying pan off the stove as smoke filled the air.

"Bagels over easy, pigs in a poke, they all taste better if they're cooked in smoke." Uncle Harry pushed the map and the hamster drawing aside and put three plates on the table.

"Come on, boys. Let's eat. Then we'll take a little hike."

"A hike?" asked Jake.

"Sure," said Uncle Harry. "There's only one way to find out about that Ogre, isn't there?

IZZY

FRISKE

MAP FOR
FINDING OGRES

hill

Sam, don't forget to bring your key."

"Why does the Ogre need the key?" Sam asked.

"I wonder," said Uncle Harry.

"I bet you do," said Jake.

CHAPTER
SEVEN

"Backpack?" Uncle Harry asked.

"Backpack," Jake answered.

"Band-Aids?" Uncle Harry asked.

"Band-Aids," Jake answered.

"Water?" Uncle Harry asked.

"Water," Jake answered.

"Let me do one," said Sam.

"Key?" Uncle Harry asked, turning toward Sam.

"Key," Sam answered, loud and clear. "Hey, Uncle Harry, you forgot something," he added.

"What's that?" asked Uncle Harry.

"The map!" said Sam, jumping up and down.

"No, sir," said Uncle Harry. He slapped his shirt pocket. "No, sir, I did not forget the map.

Now *you*, sir, need to string your key on something."

Uncle Harry pulled a long leather cord out of his other shirt pocket and threaded it through the end of the key. He tied a knot and then hung the key around Sam's neck.

"He's lucky," said Jake.

"We are *all* lucky," said Uncle Harry. "How many people are there who can say they have been asked to help the Ogre? Come on, men. Forward, march!"

"Can I go first?" asked Jake.

"Of course. You *must* go first," said Uncle Harry. "You are the one who understands the Ogre. Don't you remember saying you felt sorry for him?"

"I guess so," said Jake. "I didn't mean a real ogre, though. Just the one in the story."

Uncle Harry suddenly slapped his hand against his head. "Zounds!" he cried. "I completely forgot!" He looked at his watch. "I have an audition this morning. I'll have just enough time to drive into the city if I leave right this minute."

He pulled out the map and handed it to

Jake. "Guard this map with your life, Jake. And stay on the path to the tree house. I'll be back as soon as I can. Good luck, boys. I hope you find the Ogre."

Uncle Harry gave each boy a quick pat on the head. Then he rushed out the door, jumped into his car, and sped down the driveway.

Jake and Sam stared at each other.

"Do you think he should have left us like that?" Sam asked. "He's supposed to be taking care of us. And what's an addition?"

"*Audition*, dummy. He acts out stuff and then he gets to be in a play if people like him." Jake sighed. "I guess it's important, or he wouldn't have gone."

"Are we still going to find the Ogre?" Sam asked in a small voice.

Jake sighed again. "Sure," he said. "We've been to the tree house millions of times."

"You don't really believe the Ogre is there, do you?" asked Sam. "You think this is dumb."

"There's only one way to find out if the Ogre is there," said Jake. He made his voice deep, like Uncle Harry's. "Come on, man, forward . . . *march!*"

Jake pushed open the door and headed for the woods. Sam followed.

They scrambled up the steep hillside behind the house. They climbed over large, mossy boulders. They climbed under prickly pine branches. They stepped in squishy places where small animals lived. And Sam did not complain once.

Then Jake stopped. He looked around, shading his eyes with his hands, like a scout. "Sam, I don't see the woodpecker tree," he said.

"There," Sam said, pointing. "There it is."

"Oh, yeah," said Jake. "Good job, Sam."

"And there's the rock with all that curly stuff growing on it," said Sam as they climbed higher.

"And there's the tree house," said Jake. He stared up at the tall tree. The wind whooshed through its branches. Crows cawed. Jake shuddered.

"Do you think there really *could* be an ogre in there?" he asked.

CHAPTER EIGHT

Sam clutched the key that hung around his neck. His eyes filled with tears. He sat down on the ground in front of the tree house with a thud.

"It's *my* key," he wailed. "It's not *his* key. The Tooth Fairy gave it to *me*."

"The Tooth Fairy never said it was your key," Jake told him. "She told you it belonged to the Ogre."

Sam's cheeks were bright pink from climbing up the hill. Now they turned even pinker. "I hate the Tooth Fairy. She can't give me something and then take it away." Sam began to kick his feet. "I'm not going to give it to you," he called up to the tree house. "Not even if you eat me up."

"Don't say that," Jake said. He knelt down beside Sam and whispered, "How come that old Ogre is up there, anyway? I thought he got turned into a mouse and was eaten up by Puss in Boots."

Sam thought about this. "Yeah," he whispered back. "That's right."

"Unless Puss in Boots didn't eat him. Maybe he just ran away, like my hamsters."

"But then why didn't he turn back into an ogre and kick Puss and everybody else out of his castle?"

Jake and Sam sat and shook their heads. They couldn't puzzle it out. After awhile, Jake asked, "Are we going up there or not?"

"I guess we have to," Sam said. He pulled the key away from his neck and held it in his hand. "The Tooth Fairy said he needs the key very badly."

Jake stood up and hitched up his backpack. "Okay," he said. "Are you ready?"

Sam stood up and wiped the tears and prickly sweat off his face with the inside of his sleeve. "Can I have something to drink first? I'm thirsty."

Jake pulled off his backpack. He opened it, took out the water bottle, and handed it to Sam.

"I'm hungry," said Sam, after he had drunk half the water in the bottle. "Why didn't we bring anything to eat?"

"Come *on!*" cried Jake. He snatched the water bottle away from Sam, capped it, and shoved it back into his backpack. Then he started to walk toward the tree house.

"There's no such thing as an ogre," he said.

But his legs were shaking. His hands were sweaty. His arms didn't want to bend.

Step over step, hand over hand, Jake and Sam climbed up the tree house ladder. Holding his breath, Jake pushed open the tree house door.

There was nothing. No Ogre. Jake let out his breath and walked in. No sign of an ogre. Just the table and chairs and the old lemonade pitcher and the broken cups.

But in the middle of the table was a small cage.

Sam burst into the tree house and rushed over to the cage. "Jake! Jake!" he shouted. "There's a mouse in here!"

Jake stood behind Sam and looked in the

cage. Sure enough, there was a little black mouse.

Jake and Sam looked at each other. They looked back down at the mouse.

"I bet I know who this mouse is," said Sam.

"Oh, come on, you don't really think . . ."

"Of course I do," said Sam. "Remember, the Ogre turned into a mouse."

"But how did he get here?" Jake asked.

"Someone put him here," said Sam.

"*Someone*," Jake said. "I bet I know who."

He opened the cage and slowly curled his fingers around the mouse. Its little nose and ears and whiskers twitched.

"Look, he's winking at me," Jake said. He held the mouse close to his face. "He's so warm. And I can feel his little heart beating."

"Can I hold him?" Sam asked.

"Sit on the floor," Jake said. "And don't drop him."

Sam sat on the floor. He cupped his hands, and Jake handed him the mouse.

Then Sam screamed.

CHAPTER
NINE

"Jake! Jake!" Sam shouted. "He's growing, Jake. He's turning back into an ogre!"

Sam flung the mouse at Jake. Jake quickly put it back into the cage and shut the door.

Sam lay flat on his back. "Whew!" he said. "That was a close one."

Jake stared at the mouse. "Are you *sure* he was getting bigger?"

"Of course I'm sure," Sam said. "Don't you believe me?"

"I don't know," said Jake. "I don't know what to believe anymore."

Sam jumped up. "Well, here's his old key. I'm going home to get something to eat." He slipped the leather cord over his head. Then he opened the cage and put the key next to the mouse.

"I don't think we should leave him here," said Jake. "He's probably hungry, too. We'll have to carry him back down the hill."

"What if he turns back into an ogre while we're carrying him?" asked Sam.

Jake thought a moment. Then he picked up the cage and started to walk out the door. "Then *he* can carry *us*."

Jake carried the mouse for awhile. Then Sam carried him. He tried to be careful, but now and then he knocked the cage against trees and rocks.

"I can't wait to show him to Uncle Harry," said Sam.

"I can't wait to get something to eat," said Jake. "Look, Uncle Harry is back. His car is in the driveway."

"Good," said Sam. "We can show Uncle Harry the Ogre *and* get something to eat."

"Uncle Harry! Uncle Harry!" the boys yelled as they burst into the house. "Uncle Harry, look who we found!"

Uncle Harry inspected the cage and the mouse. "Boys, what a splendid deed you have

done!" he exclaimed. "You have gone out into the wilds and brought back the Ogre. And all on your own!"

"Why would an ogre want to be a mouse in a cage?" Jake asked. "That's dumb. If he were an ogre, he could break those little bars like spaghetti."

"Don't talk about food," said Sam. "I'm hungry."

"Then you shall eat!" said Uncle Harry. "We'll feast on homemade pizza. And then we'll tell our tales."

After they'd eaten every last bite of the pizza—and polished off strawberry ice-cream cones, too—Uncle Harry and the boys gathered around the cage. They all stared at the black mouse.

"He's so little and cute," Jake said. "It's hard to believe he's really an ogre."

"I bet that's why he needs the key," said Sam. "I bet he can't turn back into an ogre unless he has that key."

Everyone stared at the gold key in the mouse's cage. Just then, the mouse tugged on the leather cord with his tiny teeth.

"See," said Sam excitedly. "He's trying to pull the key toward him. He's going to turn into an ogre right before our eyes!"

Suddenly Sam leaped toward the cage. "I'm taking the key out!" he cried. "It's *my* key, and I want it. I could turn into a dog with this key. I've always wanted to be a dog!"

Sam opened the door to the cage. His fingers grabbed for the key, and in that moment, the mouse ran out of the cage and the key went flying. And because everyone was looking for the mouse, no one saw where the key landed.

CHAPTER TEN

Jake and Sam and Uncle Harry fell to the floor.

"Where's the mouse?" Jake cried.

"Where's my key?" Sam wailed.

"Where, oh, where, is my sanity?" Uncle Harry asked.

And then there was a shout of joy from Jake. "I found them!"

"Them?" asked Uncle Harry. "The mouse *and* the key?"

"Frisky and Lazy!" said Jake. "The picture must have worked, Uncle Harry. They're right in this corner, under the sink." Jake scooped up his hamsters and held them carefully against his chest.

"Well, I'll be!" said Uncle Harry. "Frisky and

Lazy, I am so pleased to meet you." He gently shook each hamster's paw.

"But we didn't find the Ogre or my key," said Sam. His mouth was pulled into a sad frown.

They all crawled on the floor again and looked some more. Finally Uncle Harry stretched the crick out of his neck and stood up. "Come on, boys. Let's stop for a while. With any luck, the mouse will find the key by himself and go back to being an ogre or whatever he wants to be."

"That doesn't help me," said Sam. Then his face brightened. "I know what we can do! We can get the Tooth Fairy to come back here. She was supposed to give me something, and she never did, you know."

"Why would she come back?" Jake asked. "You didn't lose another tooth."

"I can put a piece of macaroni under my pillow, and it will look like a tooth. Won't it, Uncle Harry?"

"That would be like lying," Jake said. He was pouring hamster treats into the hamsters' cage.

"Well, maybe it would be okay this one time," said Uncle Harry. "Just don't make a habit of it. I heard the Tooth Fairy takes the teeth she collects

and gives them to babies for their new teeth. Imagine if *you* were a baby and got macaroni teeth."

"Macaroni teeth!" Sam crashed to the floor and began to laugh. Jake fell on top of him and they began to wrestle. Uncle Harry joined them, and the three of them wrestled all afternoon. It wasn't long before it was time for supper.

CHAPTER
ELEVEN

By a vote of three to zero, they had Slumgoni for supper.

"Slumgoni is my one and only," Uncle Harry sang. "Hamburgini with a teeny bit of tomato sauce, add oodles to the noodles, and what do you have? Oh, my honey, oh, Slumgoni!"

And then it was bedtime. Sam smashed a piece of uncooked macaroni with his shoe and chose the bit that looked most like a tooth.

"I hope the Tooth Fairy doesn't get mad," said Sam, putting the bit of macaroni under his pillow. "Maybe you could write her a note, Uncle Harry."

Sam found a piece of paper and a pencil and handed them to Uncle Harry. "This is what I want you to say. 'Dear Tooth Fairy. Don't be mad about the macaroni tooth. We gave the Ogre the key, like you said. But we lost the Ogre. And the key. This time, give me something for me. Your friend, Sam.'"

Uncle Harry wrote down everything Sam said and put the note under Sam's pillow, next to the macaroni tooth.

"Do you want me to read *Puss in Boots* to you tonight?" Uncle Harry asked.

"Act it out again," said Jake.

So Uncle Harry leaped around the room, playing all the parts. He played the miller's son and Puss, the King and the Princess. And, of course, he played the Ogre.

When he got to the part about the Ogre turning into a mouse, Sam said, "Don't let the cat eat him up. Have him run into a mouse hole or something."

So, this time, when the Ogre became a mouse, Uncle Harry squeezed under the bunk bed. Then he puffed his way out and jumped to his feet and became Puss again.

"Shucks!" he said, snapping his fingers. "I couldn't catch that mouse. *Now* what will I do?"

"I like that ending better," said Jake.

"Now it's time for the quiet of night," said Uncle Harry. "The Tooth Fairy only comes at the quiet of night." He grabbed Sam and tossed him into his bed. He chased Jake until he caught him and threw him up to the top bunk.

"Sing us a song before you go," said Sam.

"On the night of Slumgoni, our slumber is deep," Uncle Harry sang. "Sleep, little ones, sleep, little ones, sleep, little ones, sleep."

"Uncle Harry?" Sam asked. "How was the addition?"

"He means the *audition*," said Jake.

"Very good," Uncle Harry said. "I think I got the part."

"What part?" asked Sam.

"I may play the part of an ogre," said Uncle Harry.

"Really?" both boys asked.

"Really," Uncle Harry said. "Now go to sleep."

"I'm not sleepy," said Jake. "Tell me another story about when you and Mom were kids."

Uncle Harry pulled himself up onto Jake's bed. "Your mom and I used to put on plays," he said. "She was older, so she'd play the Queen and

I'd have to play her slave. Your mom sure liked to boss me around."

"That's what's good about being the oldest," said Jake. "Did you ever get to play the King and make Mom be your slave?"

"Once," said Uncle Harry with a smile. "I baked a cake and made your mom eat it."

"Was it good?" asked Jake.

"It was great," said Uncle Harry. "It had about half a gallon of vinegar in it."

"Good idea," said Jake. "Maybe I'll make a cake like that for Sam tomorrow. And I'm going to draw a picture of the mouse so he'll come back, like the hamsters did."

"Unless he's already an ogre," said Uncle Harry, swinging down off the bunk.

"Uncle Harry . . ." said Jake.

"Good night, Jake," said Uncle Harry as he walked out of the room. "And may your dreams be merry!"

CHAPTER
TWELVE

In the quiet of night Jake awoke from a deep sleep. There were voices in the hallway.

"Rosalind," he heard a deep, growly voice say.

"Oscar," a soft, sweet voice answered.

"I found the key," said Oscar.

"So I see," said Rosalind.

Jake slowly slid down the bunk ladder. As quietly as he could, he groped his way onto his brother's bed. His heart almost stopped when Sam grabbed him.

"Jake!" Sam squeaked. "Do you hear that? They're right outside the door!"

"Shh," said Jake. "If they know we're awake, they'll go away."

"Rosalind," the growly voice said. "Why did you decide to help me?"

"I felt sorry for you," said Rosalind. "The cat and the miller's son just moved in on you. And I knew you weren't a bad ogre. After all, I've known you for a long time—ever since you lost your first tooth. I knew you were just mean because your boots were too tight."

"I'm embarrassed to tell you this," Oscar began shyly. "But I liked being a mouse. I mean, I liked it when that older boy was taking care of me. It was much nicer than being a grumpy ogre."

Sam squeezed Jake's hand.

"Well, Oscar," said Rosalind, "there is something you can do about that."

"I know," growled Oscar. "And I *am* going to do it. Then you can give this back to the younger boy."

There was a sort of thumping noise. Jake wanted to go out and see what was going on. But before he could move, the bedroom door began to open.

The boys lay frozen, scarcely daring to breathe. A shadowy figure entered the room—a tall figure in a floppy hat and robe.

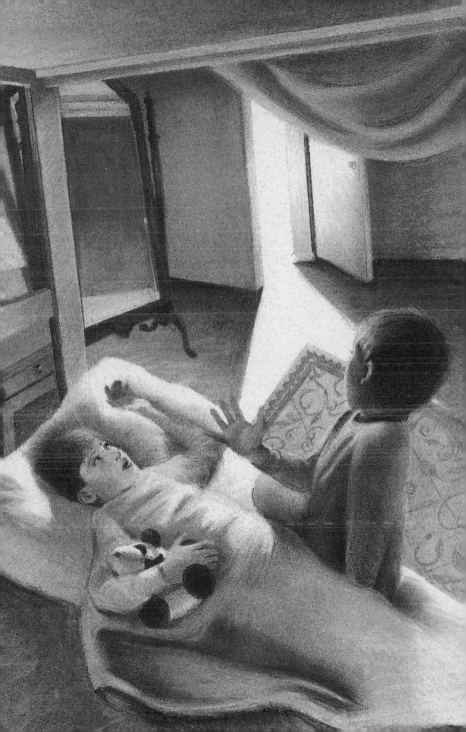

The figure stood beside the bunk. It bent down and reached under Sam's pillow. It found the note. "Macaroni," it whispered with a chuckle.

Something was put under the pillow. Then the shadowy figure straightened and tiptoed out of the room.

Sam sat straight up in bed. His hand slid under his pillow and came out holding . . . the gold key.

"The Ogre gave it back to me," Sam whispered. He shut his eyes tight. "I wish . . . I wish . . ."

Jake waited, wishing with him. But Sam did not turn into a dog.

"I'm sorry," Jake said.

"It's okay," said Sam. "I knew it wouldn't work. I guess the magic of the key is just for the Ogre."

Jake flew out of bed. He ran out of the bedroom and slid down the banister. Sam was right behind him, the gold key in his hand.

And there, in the kitchen, with moonlight streaming in, was the cage . . . with the black mouse inside it.

Jake opened the cage and cupped the mouse in his hands. He held him close and whispered, "Hello, Oscar."

Uncle Harry came in. He looked rumpled in his striped pajamas. "What's going on?" he asked.

The boys told him about Oscar and Rosalind and showed him the mouse and the key. "How splendid!" Uncle Harry said.

Jake tapped Uncle Harry on the arm. "When you went to that audition, are you sure you didn't get *two* parts?"

Uncle Harry shook his head. "I'll tell you something about acting, Jake," he said. "A good actor doesn't just pretend. He *believes*. And that's what you can do."

"Well, I believe Oscar is the best mouse in the whole world," said Jake with a smile. "How's that for a start?"

"Excellent," said Uncle Harry. "This calls for a midnight feast. What shall we have?"

"Chocolate," said Jake.

"Cherries," said Sam.

"Chocolate-covered cherries," said Uncle Harry.

And so, on that evening of moonlight and mouse and magic, the story of Jake and Sam and the Ogre comes to an end.